Frozen Time

Sam Kissinger

For Jessica, Jackson, and Louis.

I wrote this story in 2006, on a backpacking trip through Europe. Thousands of years of art and poetry amalgamated into what follows. It is 100% written by me.

This story is illustrated with AI generated art. I understand the ethical dilemma behind AI art. I am not using it as a gimmick. I'm using it for three reasons. The first is that I am a talentless visual artist.

Second, high quality artists are expensive. Having seen the creative process of excellent visual artists, they deserve their rate. My hope is to reissue this book with a human illustrator (so buy more copies!). In addition to taking away work opportunities, AI art copies styles. To avoid this I have prompted each image to emulate the styles of artists in the public domain.

The third reason I'm using generative AI art is because I like the juxtaposition of a cutting edge technology supporting the story of the two most ancient entities on our planet.

By definition, AI art lacks humanity. The act of creating is a struggle, and that struggle creates connection. There is no emotional connection between AI and its work, and this can make it hard for the viewer to connect to the art. I find this lack of connection intriguing, because I find some of these images stirring. I don't know what that says about me.

As an additional treat, try finding the oddities of each composition, such as extra fingers, disjointed limbs, and odd expressions. If this poem inspires you to create, please share your art with me and the world using #frozentime on your favorite social media platform.

I hope you enjoy this story as much as I do.

With sincere gratitude,

Sam Kissinger

Mother Nature and Father Time sat upon a lush green.
He looked at her and said: "This is like an ageless dream."
Smiling to him, she blew a kiss and Time's hands wrapped around her,
"Eternity," said he, "Cannot divide us asunder."
"And so we shall," said the Lady, "Be forever together."
They smiled now as butterflies flitted through the heather.
A warm breeze blew and shook the leaves, as petals showered ground;
Then suddenly, in the distance, there was a frightful sound.

Out on the horizon, they saw a storm approaching fast.
A hideous laugh loudly rang; the lovers were aghast.
Hail and snow pelted the ground, trees fell, mountains shattered;
Icy ruin engulfed the earth, leaving Nature tattered.
They knew who the villain was at once, but had doubted his threats,
Now, they watched in horror as the monster's frozen plague spread.

Then swiftly from out of the sky, a tall, white figure emerged.
Bearded, with a rough, haughty laugh, he coldly spoke these words:
"Mother, your power will be mine--Father step aside.
My vengeance shall strike you down, if you will not abide.
Earth will be Winter's dominion, I've come to take the throne,
I'm giving you a fair deal, so you can save your crone.
Leave at once and Nature will be spared. Or fight me and suffer.
The choice is yours to make right now, the safe way or the rougher?
The consequence shall sweep the globe, with you left powerless.
Terror will reign because of me and Earth left flowerless."

Nature tried hard to choke back tears, as Time stood standing still.
He looked around at the ruin, hearing his love's cries—shrill.
Leave to spare Nature's creation, or fight for his love's hand?
He would resist Winter's orders and fight to his last strand.

Nature said, "Time, I will go to spare us both the battle,
And quiet our misguided son, who just wants to prattle."

Knowing all wounds were his to heal, Time caressed Nature's face.
Looking deeply into her eyes, he calmly made his case;
"Nature, dear, please do not worry, we shall remain just fine.
Our boy is no match for me, he'll wither on the vine."

He kissed her gently on the cheek and turned to his rival.
A cold wind blew across his face, the intensity was primal.

Each was poised ready to attack, each waiting to explode.
Suddenly, Time leaped at Winter, he was feeling very bold.
Winter rolled, then regained his feet, and held his staff aloft,
He cast a spell and hail stones rained, but Time just simply scoffed.

Then Time's hands made such a motion, making his next attack,
That Winter knew what move coming, so he could counteract.
His staff came up and struck a blow, Time fell to Winter's heels.
Winter laughed a moment saying, "Time's character revealed.
I've put you in your place Father, there's nothing you can do.
You are helpless to stop me, I'm successful in my coup.

"I have the other seasons, so you are without aid.
Rise again, and Spring will suffer, following this raid."

Time coughed icy pain, trying for another round.
He saw the fear in Nature's eyes as she clutched her tattered gown.
He knew that he must save her, but saw no safe way now,
Rising, he drew in the cold air and took his final bow.

"I do this not for you Winter, but for my one true love.
I will not yield but will not fight, there is no peace--no dove.
Do your worst and I will receive, but know this from the start,
Nature's strength is enduring, she's always in my heart.
I am permanent--infinite--and I will not forget
The pain that you have caused us here, I'll still win this tête-à-tête."

Sobbing, Nature fell to her knees; with each wail the sky broke.
A wide smile crossed Winter's face, approaching Time, he spoke,
"You're more a fool than I had thought, and a coward to boot.
I'll reign for millennia while you will turn to soot."

"Son," Time said, "You may call yourself Old Man, but you act infantile.
Do not let your guard down, for I will see you in a while."

Winter replied, "You're no match for me and you cannot defend.
Your reign is over, I'm the king. Your death—a fitting end."
He stepped back now, his piece was said. He prepared his death-knell.
"Nature," Time called, "Take my strength--take from me like a well."

"I love you!" was all she could say when sleet began to fall.
Ice engulfed Time, muffling his cries behind a frosty pall.
Snow drifts then rose to bury him deep inside an icy grave,
As Winter looked on gleefully, now with the power that he craved.
Dominion over Earth was his. He would do as he saw fit,
And he would let all creatures know that he ruled all of it.

After the last flake had fallen, locking the frozen cell,
Winter finally ruled Nature, barely having cast a spell.
He built a palace of ice; set Time's crown high on his own head,
Then went to tell the animals that soon they'd all be dead.

His reign would be historic, an eon of despair.
Using ice to carry boulders, the crust was his to pare.
Cutting, scraping, ripping, changing--through these he released his rage.
Ever Winter would be known as the King of the Ice Age.

Back at Winter's palace, the Queen mulled her future,
Thinking of her lost true love--the cut she couldn't suture.
Animals brought her tales of their torture and their pain,
This to her was no surprise, she was going through the same.
Winter's frosty fist had Nature and the seasons in his clutches,
Still she tried to find a way to bring Winter to justice.

Each night, she'd slip out and try to dig Time free.
With bloodied, frozen fingers, working endlessly.
Her tears would freeze upon her face, boring into the icy crypt.
Each morning she'd leave some of herself; red roses as a gift.

She knew his freedom was a hopeless illusion,
Despair pushed Nature close to the edge of ruin.

Gazing through the azure panes, she'd wish for Time's release.
But soon it became too much to wish, her heart needed some peace.

As each day passed her by, she eventually stopped.
Time became a memory, (a mindset most adopt.)
She forgot that Time existed, the days just seemed to pass.
She finally gave into Winter--until she saw a blade of grass.

Suddenly, hope came flooding back, thinking of her lost Time.
Through ages she'd forgotten him, it seemed a dreadful crime.
She ran, clandestine, to his crypt to gaze on him once more.
And what she found when she arrived was a hole, like a door.
She went through to look for Time, growing colder as she went.
Could he have survived this cell? It would have been torment.
She heard a crack behind her and thought it would give way,
She turned to run but stopped again, gasping in dismay.

Emotion welled as she looked on, unsure of what to do.
No place to run, no place to hide, her face changed many hues.

At the end of the icy hall, was the face that she feared most.
She hid herself behind her hands, the figure inching close.

An icy blast obscured her sight, billowing frozen smoke.
She cowered down while trembling, her scream became a choke.
Nature shed a single tear, and watched it fall to earth.
And when it touched the icy ground, she witnessed a rebirth.

Surprise struck her like lightning, emotions ran in torrents.
Long had she been hoping for -- and fearing -- this occurrence.
From 'neith the snow came shooting forth an abundance of growth.
Then looking up, to her surprise, Time knelt offering his troth.

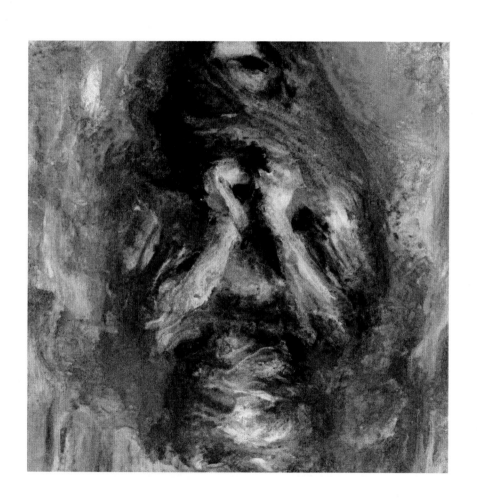

She could not look him in the eye, yet could not look away,
Her heart quaked and breath gusted as she gathered strength to say:
"I do not understand this Time, how could you have gotten free?
But most of all, what I don't get, how could you still love me?
I should have fought and sacrificed, just like you did for us.
All I could do was hear your pain and give you one last buss.
I left you 'lone for all those years, I forgot about you.
Now here you are, hand extended--I should never doubt you."

She wiped her tears and then embraced the man of all her dreams.
Then she said, looking in his eyes, "I'm sorry that it seems
That I could not withstand the pain but it was far too great.
After your capture I did try hard to escape.
But Winter locked me in my chamber, and coldly menaced me.
Saying if I bowed to him, and then he would let me be.
I secretly came here and wept, under cover of night.
As eons passed after his conquest, he began to treat me right.
I was fed, robed in fine cloth, given diamonds of ice.
And so I gave in to Winter, while you suffered the price."

Now Nature wept, pouring out guilt and pain of forgetting.
But Time chuckled softly and said, "It's not worth regretting.
What you did was for the best, so set your heart at ease.
My greatest fear wasn't death, but that both our hearts would freeze.
On your guilt of forgetting me, please rest easy my dear.
You too were a prisoner while I was trapped in here.
I worried not for your return, or for my memory,
The love we share was in my heart. Its fire set me free.
It kept me going through the years, now I reap the spoils.
So let us march upon the Beast, make him taste the soil."

Off they went. Nature led the way, Time stayed right behind her.
They crawled and slid, climbed over rocks, they could not be hindered.

When at last they reached the palace, Time hid himself away.
Nature stood out front and beckoned, "Winter! Come with no delay!"

Fat and slow and dumb with drink, Winter simply obliged.
He went to see the matter but to his great surprise,
He saw there was no problem there; his anger was aroused.
"I was warm, with food and drink; in no mood for 'Ah!'s and 'Wow!'s.
Why have I been summoned here? I want the reasons quick!
I need to drink up all my drunk, Time's moving! Tick, Tick, Tick!"

Suddenly a voice called out, "Your countdown has begun!
Time will always catch you, no matter how fast you run."
When the earth began to shake, Winter knew his end was near.
He tried to keep his palace together, but he was sick with fear.
A peal echoed, as jagged pieces tumbled down around him,
And when the snow had settled, only his broken dreams crowned him.

Winter lay upon his back covered in ice and rocks.
He jerked and twisted violently, but could not move the blocks.
"What is the meaning of this? You! Immediately tell.
Nature, you're behind this I see--you opened up his cell!"
Winter screamed full of rage but could not budge at all.

"It was not she," began Time, "That brought about your fall.
Listen, I'll say this once, so you can understand your role,
You cannot kill Time and Nature can't be controlled.

"Your reign is at an end, I told you I'm eternal.
Love kept me alive so long, the fire burned internal.
That is how I escaped my cell, by melting through the ice.
And now I'm here to get revenge--I'll make my stroke precise."

Winter closed his eyes, ready to receive the final blow.
Time's movements were deliberate, letting Winter's fear grow.
He lay pinned beneath the rubble, knowing his death's reason.
When Nature said suddenly "You may regain your season."

Winter's eyes opened wide on hearing this announced.
He thought ice was in his ear, or thought it mispronounced.

He looked to Time then to Nature, and could not understand,
He was pinned down motionless, and they had the upper hand.
He tried to speak, but words could not come out.

"Do not ask why," said Nature. "You can't know what we're about.
Your home will be the poles of Earth, where you will sit and wait--"
Winter thrashed to free himself but could only curse his fate.
"You'll be able to show yourself, at a time that we allow.
But until you are permitted, you'll adhere to this vow:
Never again will you trespass, to try to claim my throne.
Or saunter 'round with Time's crown, as if it is your own.
Our power is too potent and you are too weak to wield it.
The only way that this will end is for you to yield it."

Nature glared at Winter, still buried under rubble.
Surveying him with pity, but glad that he was humbled,
"False King," she said. "I will not hide that I'm disappointed.
You thought that you could take control, as if you're anointed.

"There's life on Earth we must care for, our eternal duty.
Your family cannot stand by while you dispense cruelty.

"I glad I get to tell you--your siblings have escaped,
When I found out that Time had come, there were moves to make.
Be grateful it was us here first, for they had their schemes
To pull you down from your stolen throne and tear you at the seams.

"Much consideration I put into this solution.
Your brother Summer's scorching rage sought swift retribution.
Your sister Autumn loves to see life decay and wither.
But be grateful for Spring's grace, she wanted you delivered."

Nature smiled at Winter, as he began to understand,
He was spared by the one whom he most desired damned.

"Love," Nature continued, "Is what freed Time, and saved me.
It even saved you, the one who did enslave me.

Enjoy our mercy, but remember death and pain we bring.
And know this is a far worse fate: you will now see every Spring."

The ice and snow began to melt, refilling the oceans,
As Winter sat unshackled, perceiving new emotions.
"What that's called is sadness," said Time. "It is a part of life.
All our time spent to avoid it, but know it as a fife.
It leads us into battle, or it leads us to corners.
Accept it now and be happy, or an eternal mourner."

As Winter sat listening to Time, his heart swelled with rage.
How, Winter thought, *can he spout off, lecturing like a sage?*
"You win this Time." Winter spat, "You ended my epic reign.
Revel in your victory now, but your strength will not maintain.
You may have won this battle, but will not win the war.
I'll return to finish this, so be prepared for more."
With that, in a cloud of icy air, Winter disappeared.
Time smiled and Nature chuckled as the icy dust cleared.

Time said, "He does not know, there is no end game or treasure.
We all are one, our survival and success are tethered.
Now we can go on and forget his immaturity.
And get back to where we left, marveling at purity."

They walked a little ways and then sat upon a lush green.
He looked at her and said: "This is like an ageless dream."
Smiling to him, she blew a kiss and Time's hands wrapped around her,
"Eternity," said he, "Cannot divide us asunder".
"And so we shall," said the Lady, "Be forever together."
They smiled now as butterflies flitted through the heather..
A warm breeze blew and shook the leaves as petals showered ground;
Silently, in sweet embrace, they watched the sun go down.

Made in the USA
Las Vegas, NV
01 October 2024

96082302R00029